Animals
Through the Year

Digger

Published by Raintree Steck-Vaughn Publishers, an imprint of Steck-Vaughn Company

Library of Congress Cataloging-in-Publication Data

Potter, Tessa.
Digger, the story of a mole in the fall / story by Tessa Potter; illustrations by Ken Lilly.
p.   cm. — (Animals through the year)
Summary: When torrential autumn rains flood her tunnels, Digger manages to escape from these treacherous waters only to face new danger above ground.
ISBN 0-8172-4623-1
[1. Moles (Animals) — Fiction.   2. Animals — Fiction.]
I. Lilly, Kenneth, ill.   II. Title.   III. Series.
PZ7.P8574Di   1997
[E] — dc21   96-38983
                                                                      CIP   AC

With thanks to Bernard Thornton Artists

The author would like to thank Dr. Gerald Legg of the
Booth Museum of Natural History, Brighton, for his help and advice.

Color separated in Switzerland by Photolitho AG, Offsetreproduktionen, Gossau, Zurich.

Printed and bound in the United States

1 2 3 4 5 6 7 8 9 0 IP 00 99 98 97 96

Digger

Animals Through the Year

The Story of a Mole in the Fall

Story by Tessa Potter

Illustrations by Ken Lilly

RSVP

RAINTREE
STECK-VAUGHN
PUBLISHERS
The Steck-Vaughn Company

Austin, Texas

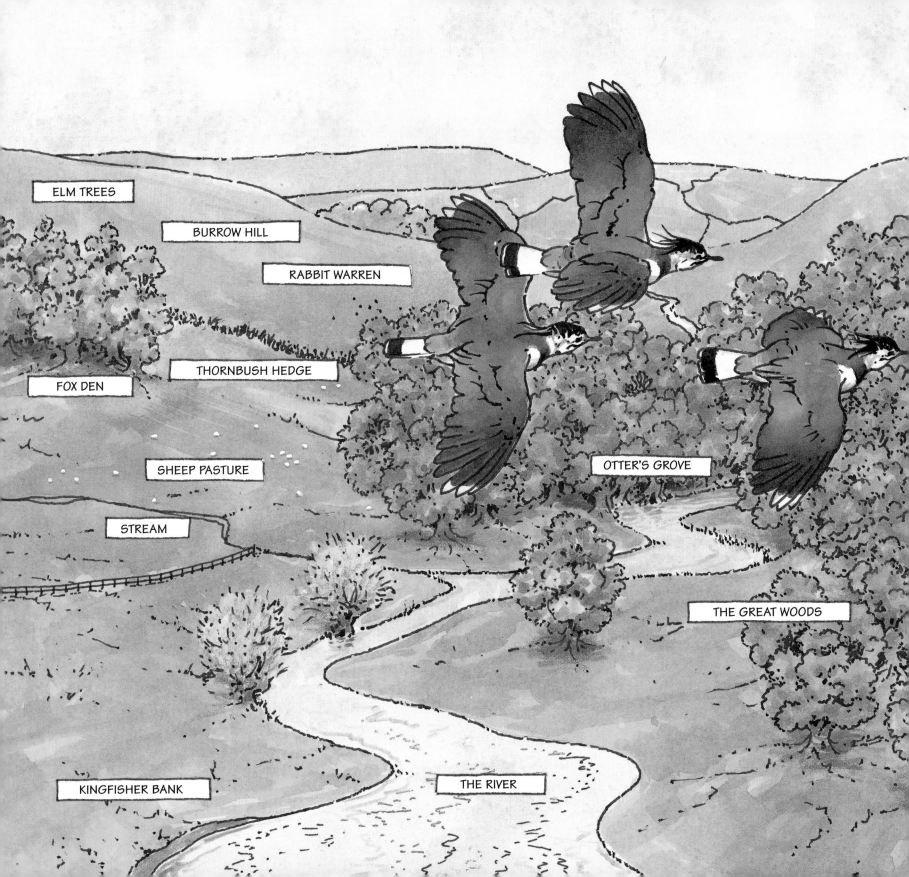

ELM TREES

BURROW HILL

RABBIT WARREN

THORNBUSH HEDGE

FOX DEN

SHEEP PASTURE

STREAM

OTTER'S GROVE

THE GREAT WOODS

KINGFISHER BANK

THE RIVER

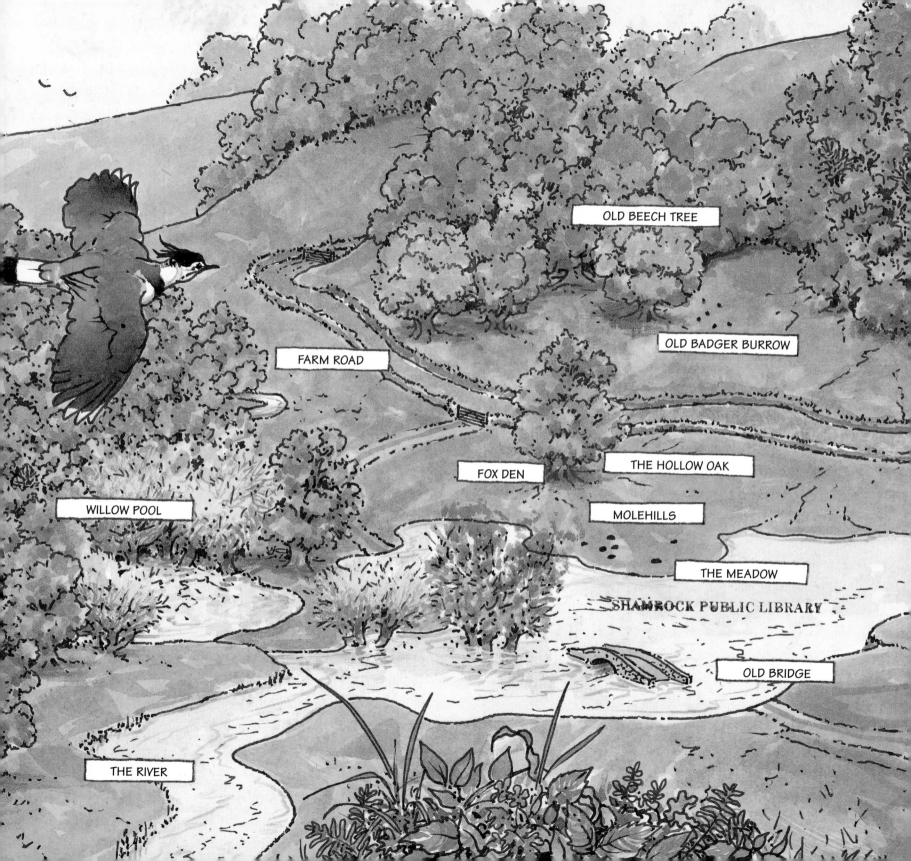

The first weeks of autumn were warm and golden. Birds feasted on the hedges while small animals searched for food, preparing for the cold months ahead. The rabbits on Burrow Hill enjoyed the last warmth of the sun.

But now the skies were dark, and a cold wind swept across the Hill, bringing rain and hail. The birds and animals took shelter where they could. A young fox took refuge in the roots of an old tree.

A young heron sat hunched on the riverbank, staring hopelessly into the swirling, muddy water. It had been raining for seven days now, and fishing was hard in the swollen river.

At last, a patch of light appeared in the sky, and the rain eased. A wagtail landed on one of the small piles of earth dotted over the meadow.

A sudden movement sent the little bird scurrying away. Fresh earth was being thrown up — Digger the mole was making a new tunnel. The rain and cold had not bothered Digger much. A little water had seeped into her tunnel, but her nest was still warm and dry.

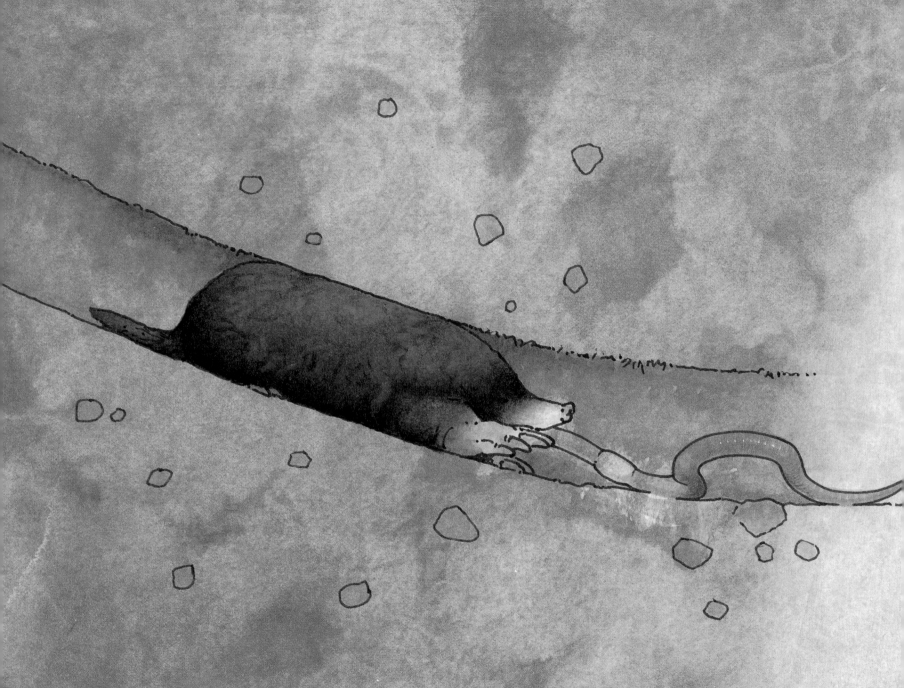

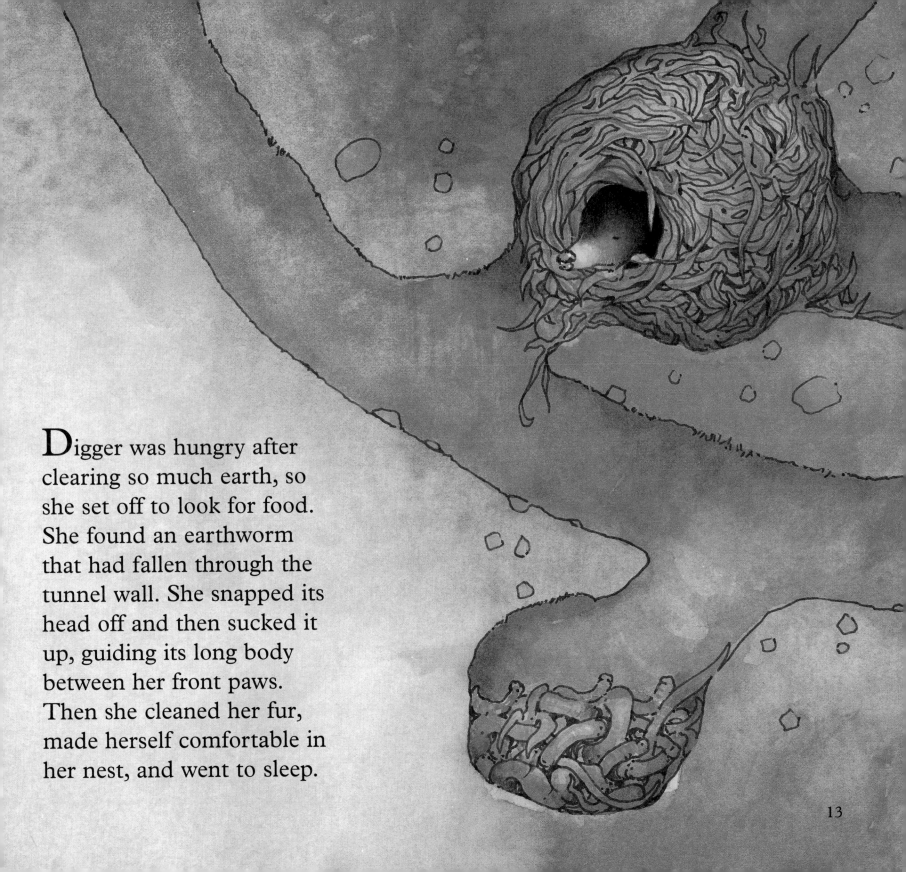

Digger was hungry after
clearing so much earth, so
she set off to look for food.
She found an earthworm
that had fallen through the
tunnel wall. She snapped its
head off and then sucked it
up, guiding its long body
between her front paws.
Then she cleaned her fur,
made herself comfortable in
her nest, and went to sleep.

13

14

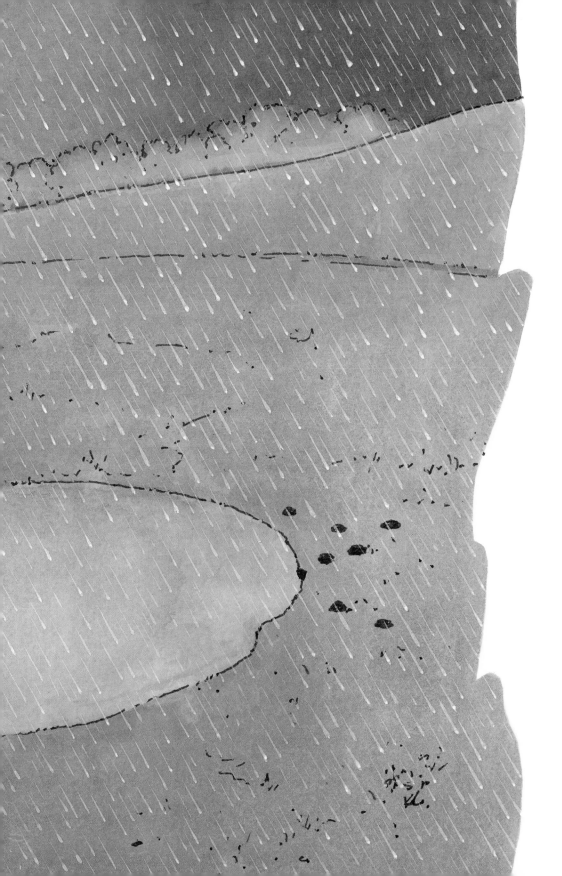

Outside, the sky had grown dark again, and huge drops of rain were falling. The heron gave up his fishing.

Then the storm broke. Lightning flashed across the sky. The wind raged, and the rain poured down in torrents. Slowly, the swirling river crept higher and higher over the reeds and rushes, until at last it broke its banks. The water swept out across the Meadow.

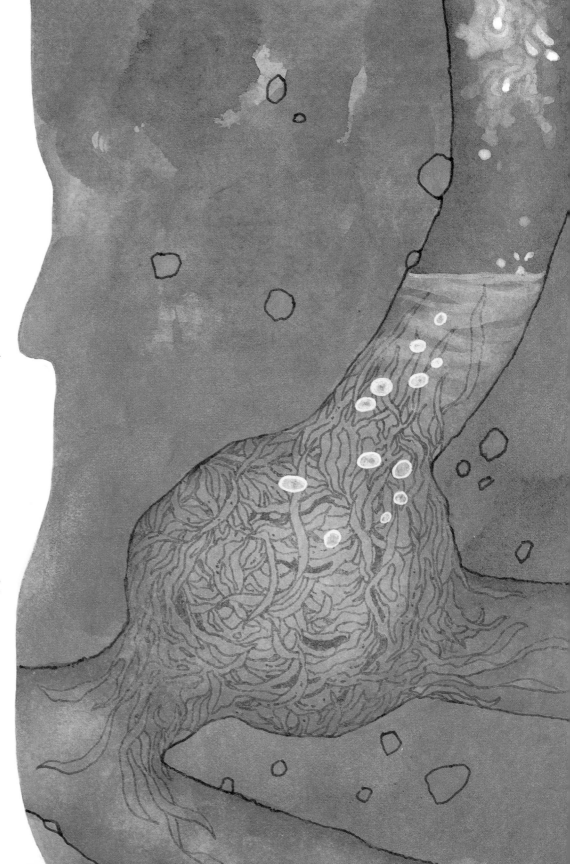

In her underground nest, Digger was woken by a trickle of water. Then, suddenly, water was roaring through her tunnels. She scrambled out of her nest and swam toward a shaft that led up to the Meadow. She had to get out. She clawed upward, trying to reach the surface, but as she pulled the earth away, more water rushed through the hole, washing her back down. She was underwater now. She couldn't breathe.

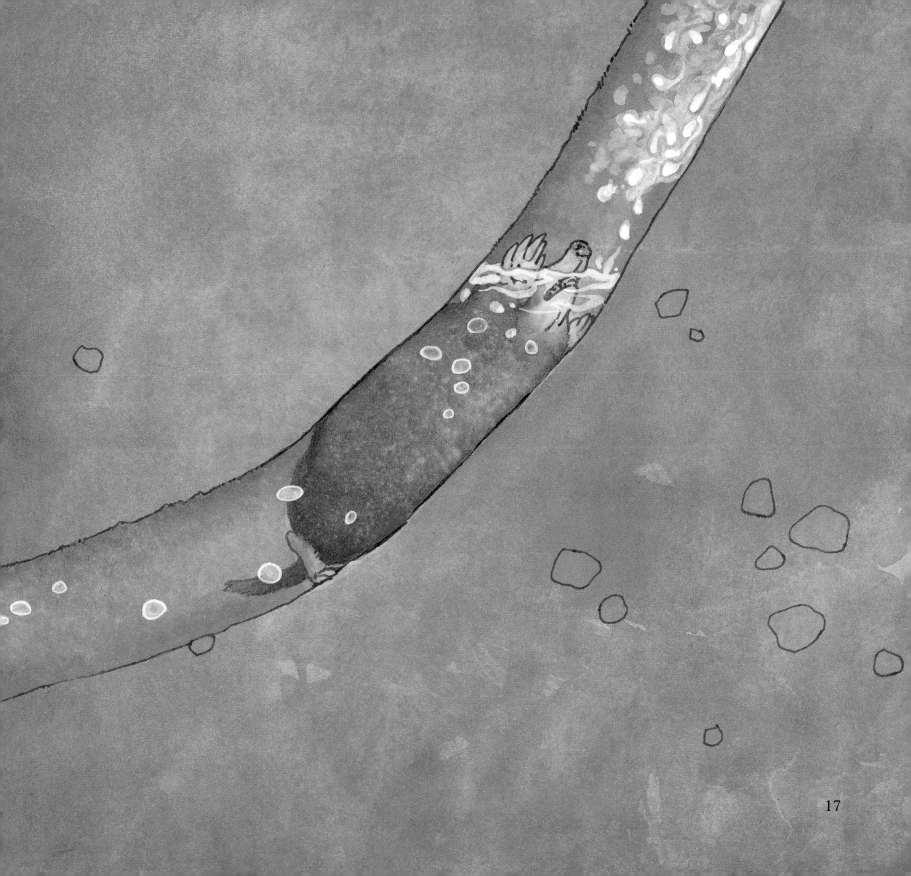

Desperately, Digger swam with her powerful front legs until, at last, she managed to pull herself up through the hole. She gulped the cold air, paddling hard to stay afloat. The whole Meadow was underwater. All around, other small creatures were trying to reach dry land.

Digger headed with all her
strength toward the high
ground. She knew that
as the wind dropped, the
hunters would appear,
looking for easy prey. For
a second, a dark shape
hovered right above her.
Digger was terrified. But
the bird turned away as
something else caught
his eye.

Finally, shivering and exhausted,
Digger dragged herself onto the land.
The heron was wading in the
shallows. He'd just caught a water shrew,
so he didn't notice Digger as
she slipped by and disappeared
into the Great Woods.

It was night when Digger woke. Everything was quiet, and the floodwater lay like a dark mirror over the Meadow. Nearby, a young otter explored the shallow water.

Digger needed food and a safe, warm shelter right away. She couldn't go back to her tunnels under the Meadow. So that night Digger set out through the Great Woods to find a new home.

Look back at the story.
Can you find...

A **vole** eating
a rosehip.

A **blackbird** eating
a blackberry.

A **split hazelnut** on the
squirrel's feeding table.

A deer mouse
carrying a hazelnut.

A **rabbit**.

A **shaggy ink cap**.

A **kestrel** hovering.

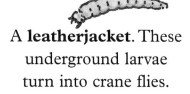

A **leatherjacket**. These
underground larvae
turn into crane flies.

A **four-spotted orb weaver spider**
in the middle of her web. If she
catches an insect, she bites it with
her fangs, and then ties it up in silk.

A **fly agaric**. This fungus
is very poisonous.

A **maple seed** spinning
to the ground.

A **common toad** hiding. The
toad will hibernate all winter.

A **gray heron** catching
a water shrew.

A **wolf spider** hunting a daddy
longlegs. The daddy longlegs
has escaped, leaving the spider
holding his wriggling leg.

A **honey mushroom**. What
animal is eating this fungus?

A **gray squirrel** eating a puffball.

An **acorn** floating in the
floodwaters. One will find its way to
soft soil, and a new tree will begin.

A **boletus**. In the autumn fungi
provide food for many animals.
In some cases, animals can eat
things that humans cannot.

An **otter**.

An **earthworm** in the mole's worm
storage. The mole bites off the
worm's head to stop it from
burrowing away.

A **hammock spider's web**.
A crane fly has bumped into
the spider's threads and fallen
into the hammock.

A **thornbush berry**.

A **water shrew** being
caught by a heron.

A **rosehip**.

THINGS TO DO

MAKING LEAF CARDS AND PICTURES. You will need pieces of cardboard, glue, a clear sheet of film called acetate, different kinds of leaves and grasses, or pressed flowers.

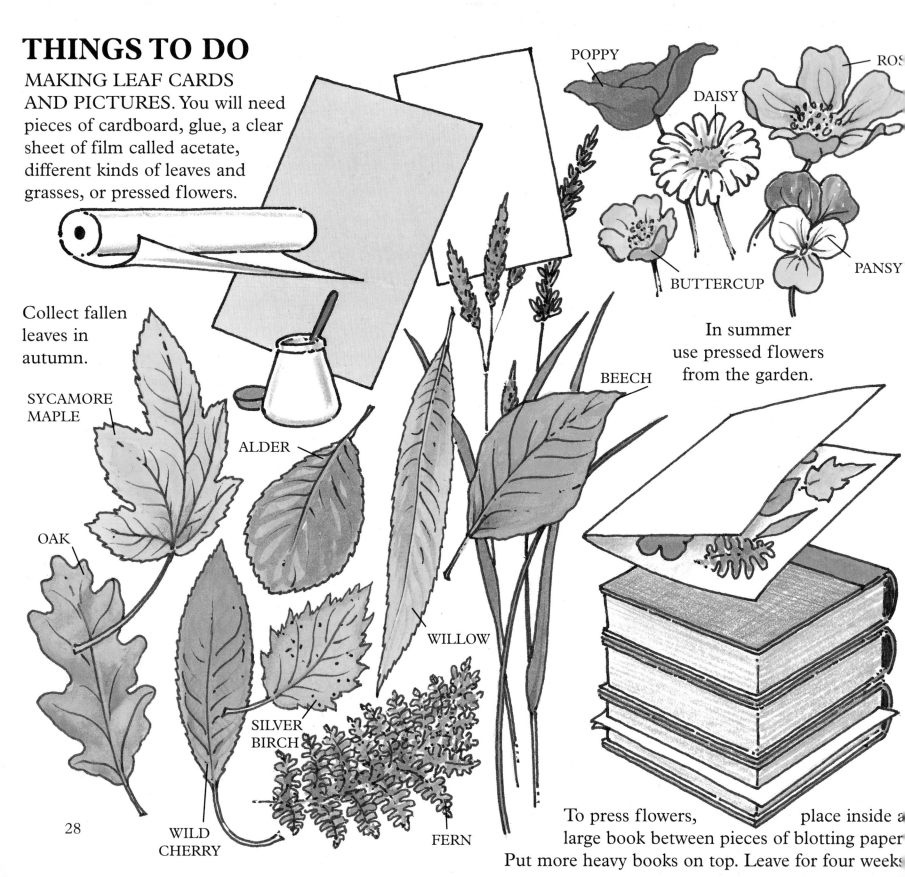

Collect fallen leaves in autumn.

In summer use pressed flowers from the garden.

POPPY

ROS

DAISY

BUTTERCUP

PANSY

SYCAMORE MAPLE

OAK

ALDER

BEECH

WILLOW

SILVER BIRCH

WILD CHERRY

FERN

To press flowers, place inside a large book between pieces of blotting paper. Put more heavy books on top. Leave for four weeks.

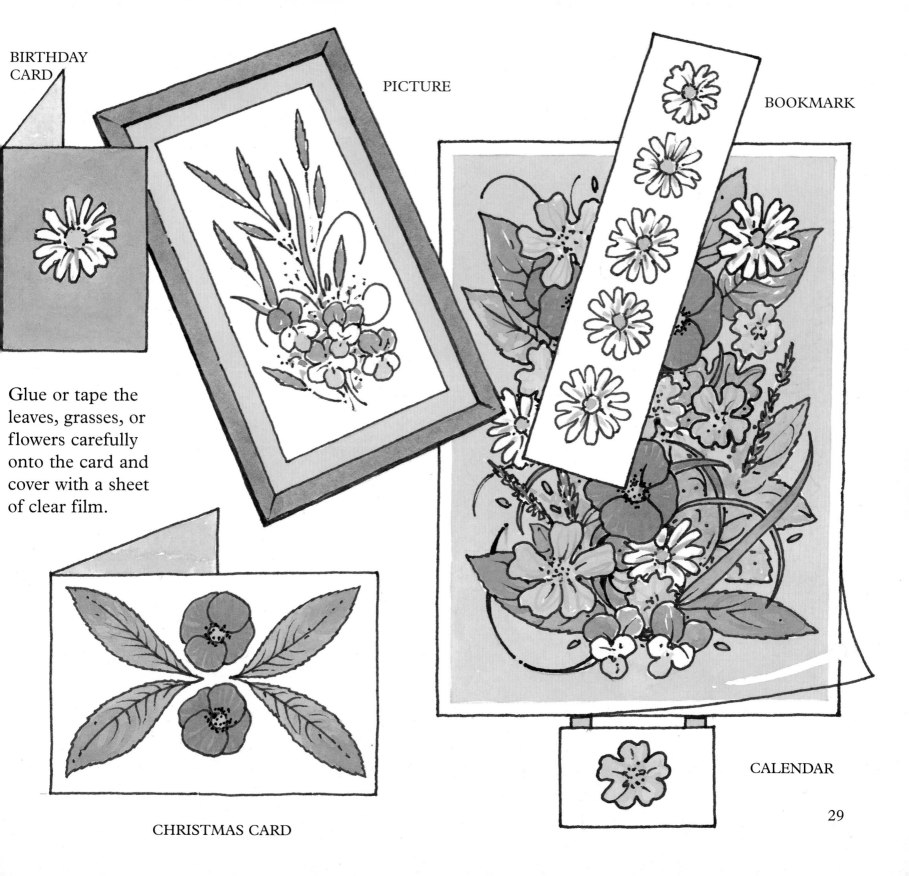

BIRTHDAY
CARD

PICTURE

BOOKMARK

Glue or tape the
leaves, grasses, or
flowers carefully
onto the card and
cover with a sheet
of clear film.

CALENDAR

CHRISTMAS CARD

29

MORE ABOUT MOLES

Books

Bailey, Jill. *Discovering Shrews, Moles, and Voles.* Watts, 1989

George, Jean C. *The Moon of the Moles.* HarperCollins Child Books, 1992

Videos

Wildlife. Dorling Kindersley, 1994

Exploring the World of Mammals. (30 min.) Busch Entertainment, Batavia, Ohio: Video Treasures, 1992

Life on Earth. Episode 10. (58 min.) BBC/Warner Brothers. Films, Inc. distributor. Naturalist David Attenborough on mammals, 1988

First published in 1996 by Andersen Press

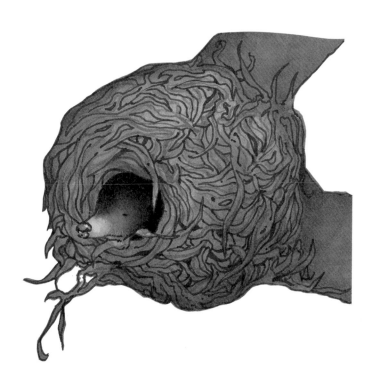